Friday
the Scaredy Cat

Playdates Are
Not Scary!

by Kara McMahon ✦ illustrated by Maddy McClellan

Ready-to-Read

Simon Spotlight
New York London Toronto Sydney New Delhi

SIMON SPOTLIGHT
An imprint of Simon & Schuster Children's Publishing Division
1230 Avenue of the Americas, New York, New York 10020
This Simon Spotlight edition July 2015
Copyright © 2015 Simon & Schuster, Inc.
All rights reserved, including the right of reproduction in whole or in part in any form.
SIMON SPOTLIGHT, READY-TO-READ, and colophon are registered trademarks of
Simon & Schuster, Inc.
For information about special discounts for bulk purchases, please contact
Simon & Schuster Special Sales at 1-866-506-1949 or business@simonandschuster.com.
Manufactured in the United States of America 0615 LAK
10 9 8 7 6 5 4 3 2 1
Library of Congress Cataloging-in-Publication Data
McMahon, Kara.
Playdates are not scary! / by Kara McMahon ; illustrated by Maddy
McClellan. — Simon Spotlight edition.
pages cm. — (Friday the scaredy cat) (Ready-to-read)
Summary: "Today is a big day! Friday has his first playdate! It is with a
nice orange cat named Mushy. There is just one problem—
Friday is scared of playdates!"— Provided by publisher.
ISBN 978-1-4814-3591-8 (trade paper : alk. paper) — ISBN 978-1-4814-3592-5
(hardcover : alk. paper) — ISBN 978-1-4814-3593-2 (eBook)
[1. Cats—Fiction. 2. Fear—Fiction. 3. Play—Fiction.] I. McClellan,
Maddy, illustrator. II. Title.
PZ7.M478752Pl 2015
[E]—dc23
2014041738

This is Friday.
He is a scaredy cat.
He is afraid of
almost everything.

Friday has a playdate today.
He has never had a playdate
before.
He is scared.

Friday decides
he will not let his
playdate come inside.
He blocks the door
with an army of mice.

The doorbell rings.
Oh no! The playdate is here!
Friday runs and hides.

He watches and waits.
Will the army of mice
keep the playdate out?

The army of mice begins
to move.
The door is opening!
The playdate must be strong!

Friday sees his playdate.
He is big! He is orange!
What kind of playdate is this?
Friday runs to a better
hiding place.

The playdate looks
for Friday.
But Friday is an expert
hider.

"Are we playing a game?"
asks the playdate.
Friday does not answer.

The playdate decides he will just play by himself.

He has a basket full of toys
that he brought to share.

Friday watches as his playdate plays with the toys. That looks like fun!

Maybe the
playdate is
not so bad
after all.

Friday creeps into
the room slowly.
He is quiet as a mouse.
His playdate keeps
playing.

Friday creeps closer.

He bumps the basket.

He spills all the toys!

Oh no!

The playdate sees Friday.
"Hello! My name is Mushy,"
he says.
Friday freezes.

"Are you mad I touched your toys?" Friday asks.

"I am not mad!" says Mushy.
"I came here to play
and share!"

Mushy bats a toy mouse
over to Friday.
"Play with me!" he says.

Friday and Mushy have so
much fun playing together.
Mushy teaches Friday some
new moves.
Friday teaches Mushy to hide.

Playdates are not scary!
Not even a little bit scary!
Friday loves his new friend.
Friday loves playdates!

"Next time we can play
at my house,"
Mushy tells Friday.
Uh-oh!
Friday is scared to go outside!